lee ranaldo's looking out the window and watching the mind-movies as they roll by. is he driving? it doesn't matter cuz what's outside seems to be driving these writings here. and what's outside seems to be stirring up his insides. by describing these "outsides," he reveals these insights on his insides. though you sense the striving to reach some manner of objectivity, some "defining power" brought on by the spectator role he's cast himself in here, the mantra of "life is not a rehearsal" echoes throughout. this is a tour of lee's head. maybe he wanted it to be one of his heart but how would I know? I like his snapshots, the way the characters are cast in confusion and missing their cues. awkward gestures making for an awkward stage manner, this is good fun and I love reading it to myself aloud. lee makes me think of myself and how I would interpret each scene, cast in such costumes. this is a gift of his and I'm grateful for him sharing it. I hear my mouth speak lee words and it's a trip. soon I'm ready to even dance like him— I'm out of control. wait, I must learn to be more academic. nope . . . maybe I shouldn't. I will cross my eyes until they double-back on each other. then you'll see . . .

–mike watt
san pedro, ca

Road Movies Lee Ranaldo
Photographs Leah Singer

Road Movies Lee Ranaldo

Photographs Leah Singer

Road Movies

Tenth Anniversary Edition
Revised and expanded Winter 2004

First Edition Spring 1994
Second Edition December 1994
Third Edition March 1997

Published by Soft Skull Press, Inc.
71 Bond St.
Brooklyn, NY 11217

ISBN 1-932360-73-5

Anniversary edition cover and layout by Don Goede
Design by Don Goede and LR/LS

Original book design by Susan Mitchell
Original Soft Skull Editorial: Sander Hicks

www.softskull.com

Selections have appeared in the following publications:
Bookstore
Half Dozen of the Other
Crossing Border Magazine
Bouillabaisse
Freedom Is...
Big Hammer
Long Shot
Bananafish

Printed in Canada

Contents

Expanded 2004

Introduction

The first time I read Road Movies ten years ago, I felt like I'd met an ally, a sort of kindred spirit and brotherly guide who embodied the necessary and vital polarities that give all good poetry that special cranial punch. This dynamic tension in Lee's poems is manifested quite adroitly by his ability to write both meditative, slippery glimpses and playful (yet serious) diatribes that tickle the brain:

mindfuck on the teeveee
says you're a jackass

It's his special ability to walk the margins that gives his work such gravity and leaves such lasting impressions (much like the slice of life photographs by Leah Singer that, while certainly independently sad and gorgeous, also act as subtle illustrations of the poems). My favorite moments in Lee's poems are when he reaches sublimely quiet heights with an eye and ear for detail that's delicately simple, elegant, and honest:

So many things now, the things that happen everyday, to everyone, are hitting me all at once.

In fact, much of his work can be read as lyrical meditations or celebrations of the solitary "I" amid the chaos and squalor of these modern (1994) times. By the same measure, Lee addresses the other extreme of this polemic by crashing head-on and fearlessly into the quivering neon meat of modern sonic life:

I'm high above the city
dreams distorting
amp thrust full
we belong here

we are safe here
something tells me
the skies are here for us
so brief
so impure

What's gratifying about these visionary moments is that they're aptly tinged with the hope that somehow we can liberate ourselves from the shit of this world enough to actually make contact (however fleeting) with something real and authentic.

Most of all, Lee has a generous spirit that manifests itself in his poems, and that lasting quality is what makes me gravitate towards these early poetic excursions. He's peered into the abyss and had the courage and compassion to write down what he's seen.

This is education! This is life, cut one frame at a time from an endless spool.

It's nice to know that Lee is living among us right now, ten years after the original publication of Road Movies. He's reading the same papers, hearing the same news, and reacting with the same horror and outrage. But still, he's moving forward with enough confidence in his words and visions to express them without caution, to embrace the life and times we live in and turn them into art that matters. That sort of bravery, grace, and diligence is remarkable in a fellow human being. So, as you scan these pages remember that not only is Lee free, but he wants all of us to be free too.

Todd Colby, NYC, 2004

Road Movies Lee Ranaldo

Photographs Leah Singer

Locusts

In a world where things fall apart
form substance and force are lost
words of violence
stalk the earth
artificial souls
feign walking edges
like a raging plague
sweeping through the fields.
Is there really a reason?
Throw out yr attics full
discard yr old loves and
yr angels in wait
throw a black cloth over it all
lock the windows
tie down the appliances
the pets
and leave it all
just lock the door
and leave

Opening

this is the longest movie
I've ever been in
nothing can alter these images
this is life like a movie
so real to the touch
injected with feelings
with no final fading

this is the same still frame
that holds us like frozen lanterns
in mid embrace
this is the movie that should last forever
always on the screen
this is the phone left off the hook

we must be responsible
and contain our movements
to a few frames on each reel
but we can freeze the image
and extinguish the sounds
of everything outside yr room
a drawn out sigh becomes the pealing of bells
yr skin an endless surface
which I will explore again and again

this is a moment which we must save
to prove such things are possible
this perfect kiss cannot be erased
tho its image may fade and bleach
what comes next doesn't matter
only this perfect, living image
shut from the world
safe in our heads

we'll live in our heads now
bright musty chambers
shut from the world
no windows open
swept under the carpet

4

New Condo

New condo
up on the hill
New credo
the rhythm method
New feeling
saved and flat and free
A new process
inside me
We move but never speak
We talk without thinking
the hot air thick
and stinking
trash everywhere
black stretch limos
unable to park
on these narrow streets

New condo
got a new condo
got a microwave
and a fashion model
got a hot sock
and a ten foot flagpole
a new word
for everything

now I'll name names
now I'll whisper a promise
to yr beautiful body

I love you
when yr nipples are hard
in the cool a/c
of my new condo
on the beautiful
gray carpet

I love you
when I'm high
and inside you
inside my new condo
inside my limo
w the smoked glass
my record collection
my fine paintings
that trompe l'oil
is the only one
of its kind

The Japanese
want my new condo
they try
to play my guitar
but their hands

are too small
they move
like the carp
they once bred
sleek and careful
full of thoughts

my new condo
is free of thoughts
it's an incredible
empty space
for me to fill
w beautiful bodies
and tasty drinks
36 inch TV's
air fresheners
these windows
don't open
this door has
three locks
w three different keys
what a pain
in my pocket
what a hard on
I have, for love
love: the idea
love: the notion
love: the good life

love: the ocean
love your hairdo, baby
love those shoes
are they Susan Bennetts?
is that real silk?
or J.C. Penny's?

dont you just love
the beautiful blue sky
up here?
a penthouse sky
is always the bluest,
truest, sky
the air seems
so rich up here
so far from the street

Put on some lipstick
bitch
you look like hell
you just ruin this place
looking like that
my new rug
covered in blood
my new windows
smudged
my new condo
shattered

my new suit
my CD player
get yr stuff
and get out
gimme back
that set of keys
and my beeper
take yr name
off the mailbox
and the charge card
this is my
new condo
mine
the red wine
all mine
don't waste my time
it's my dime
bitch
Jeesus!
Lemme get a
drink and make
a call.

Me and Jill

We had just left shore when everything began to happen at once. The water came in and we started to go down. I looked to Jill and she looked back, thinking it would be alright to go down. Then the railings broke and the motors went. The hall emptied out, no-one left for the band. The amps all wet, speakers burst. Everything soaked. We, up three flights, tried to meet up with the galley crew but it seemed everyone had gone. We had a smoke to pass some time. Jill said 'I'd love to, right now.' What could I say? We did while the waters rose, licking our feet. It was fun and funny so we laughed. I loved the way she could laugh. So full bodied.

When we hit the sky we were high over the rooves, a field of gnarled antennae coiling upwards at our feet. Waves and waveforms joining in a nice hot blast. So different from the boat. The cold silver sky opened, and we passed through.

Last I saw Jill she was heading backwards into the coils of the antennae, laughing, so beautiful. Saying she hadn't yet had her fill of the boys there and the electricity. Saying she wanted to plug in again and fry a bit. I said 'Watch the water love . . .' She kept laughing and shook her hair. She said 'I'd love to, right now, you know?' So we did and had a smoke too and her lips parted. There in amongst the coiling snakes of the antennae she looked right at home. The waves came up and a blinding flash caught me dreaming of her as she looked all crossed with wires and spikes watching the blast. Everything went orange and my thoughts dissolved in the cloud. I thought one last: how different from the sea is the boat. . . .

Richard

Richard:
yr happy alone
you tore down the world
and put up four walls
yr bleeding from every pore
yr screaming inside yr head
and you cant get me out
yr in there tonight
marshaling thoughts
you can kill the future
you can kill the past
but you cant climb out
of yr sweaty shoes
and walk away

Richard:
I never give you a thought
you've holed up
you're held up
in suspension
one too many failed tasks
one too many open roads

Clouds

less of you
thinking less of you
up under the swells
the fountain of youth
too far away to get by
on less thinking of you

code of honor
code of grace
meet me in the secret place
where i sang through you
where everything was too good
meet me there and I'll need
less thinking of you

the streets are hidden
under wings of truth
ready to reflect
and not let up
ready to reject
time's true foul up
no step you take
can stand up to
this passing of time
this hidden choice
the motel bed

soft on a rainy day
an afternoon hideout
telling some stories
finishing some things

let's take a step up
stand straight and true
what is what?
my head in tight
my hands don't touch
your skin
my body moves forward
and then back
back to which day?
back to the last time
we met
when clouds were low
and our motors ran
up and down
up and down
on the street

For Thom

the beautiful
sunny
afternoon
w blue sky
no clouds
it's late
and a crystalline
pristine
glow
holds the air

from this window ledge
where I sit
not even the trucks
rumbling
below me
can disturb it
the trees leave!
nice and green
the bldgs glint golden
hard edges of brick

now even
the trucks
have gone
leaving just
the hiss
of the
city

Hollywood

Amazing. We're here in LA now for three days. The sun is shining. The streets are clean. The morning we arrive a shiny new Chevy sportster convertible is delivered to our hotel door, courtesy of the record company, for our use. Within an hour of waking up and gazing out at the houses all stacked up on the hills of Hollywood we're in the car and the radio is on and the top is down and the sun is shining brightly and the wind is in our hair and it's sorta like a kind of paradise–one form that paradise might take: LA on a sunny morning in May. Everything sparkles and shines and all of life feels easy and you begin to wonder if this could be the kind of place one never leaves ever again. Impermeable to depression, protected from doubt beneath the green palmsway. Skins are browned here and everyone is plugged in and connected and completely out of touch with small realities like snow or cold or doubt. This edge-land of the continent bristles with a strange serene energy field and within minutes, in the car, with the radio and the sun and the streets of the strip, we fall under its spell.

Paris

She screams she screams
I am more famous than you
She lights turns through endless dreams
She's twisting her ankle
Leaning into the wind.

Step on it. Wipe the reed clean.
Inhale and don't let her breathe
She gardens in the sunlight
hiding a wise old world
She hangs on.
She hangs up.

She hangs around
then self destructs again
She'll let go and play to win
She spins, bright oxygen
Caught in my eye
Furry edged ponies in thick thatched grass
Her lace dress wrapping my head.

Time moves so fast
I cut collages on the bus from
Italian and Austrian magazines
Swam yesterday in the Spanish sea
Stood naked on the balcony,

watching the nighttime beach roll in
I could not see, but I chased images
I did not listen, or speak
My thoughts collided at midday
An unspoken truce halting logic
I could not think of you then
I think of you a lot lately
Trying for that line of sight
from me to you and back
in one easy lesson
How to stay awake?
We breathe at night
Your time is in my eye
Her place is in my heart.

Tonight is Paris
I'm stumbling, barely here
My logic, failing:
No thoughts are good thoughts
We said 'no-one can help us'
No outside world
No communication
Except maybe, somewhere, maybe . . .

Collage pictures of girls intersecting various architectures.
One advertisement diverting the next. Muscle up. All the red
lips in Marie Claire, french Vogue, Elle. The girls' magazines.
Come, come they say. That's when we really move. A plate-
ful of lips. A million kisses. Teeth hidden.

On the bus time is left behind. Everything free and easy.
Stay up til five or six a.m., wake at noon or one. It's no time
at all times. Whatever time you want it to be.

Time to sleep.
Time to look out the window.
No time to think of you.
No outside getting in.
Each moment lost to us
making way for the next.

Anything Almost, Anytime

for G.M.

Falling like a rag doll
Waiting to be caught
Eyes rolled back and crooked smile
Lost in her own world
Waiting to be scooped up

Hope she don't fall
Hope there are strong arms to guide her
when her lipsticks all smeared
and she stumbles for real
Hope she holds on
Until some sweet angel saves her
Brings her back to this world
That she knows just can't please her

Hope I can twist her hair then
And lay down so slow
Let the world run out
Keep on talking forever
Staring at the ceiling of stars

Inside that spiral chain
The world slides with excitement
We're moving through the air

I'm twisting her hair
We're speaking in tandem
A rush of emotions
Old like the oceans are old
And no-one can stop us

This Patch of Sky

I can't find you
in this patch of sky
a soldier, and epitaph, an island in the heat
the matrix of yr delight, remember?
you at the window
me at the door
forever in debt
checking the stove
who wants in?

a dragstrip
a striptease
eyes meant to please you
a spider inside you
two steps away
your present is a mess
a collar
a chokechain
a hung down ceiling
you waited all day
and couldn't say the word

we're here when you come up
we chameleon yr seven seas
on St. Marks Place the war is never over

I saw you there
getting louder as I watched
bigger, so far away
your friends in the record store, laughing

Smoke Ring

Right now we're in northern California traveling through dusty valleys ringed by tall peaks. An ancient feeling to the movement of the car—as if hurtling down and endless moibius strip of hiway, the same moods, same golden dusts and strips of land go by again and again. We settle comfortably into a timeless niche: a hard fact on the freeway. We, mute, static, looking over eternal world planet. I'll see you when we break free of this void . . .

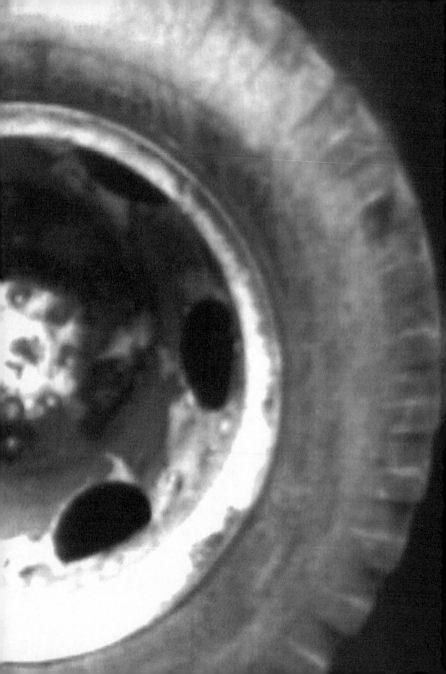

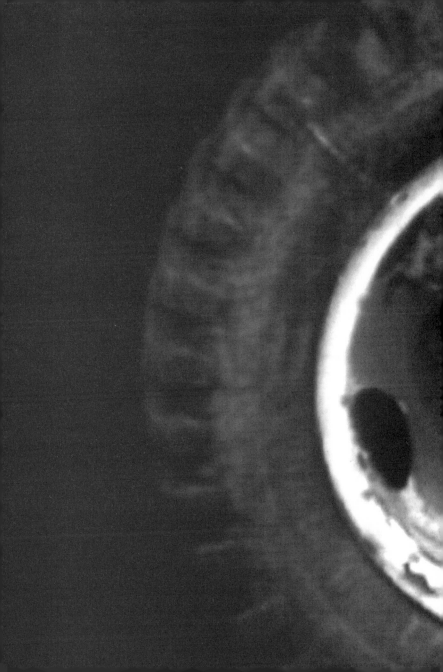

L.A.: Falling, Gleaming

the dinner party
the cement canyons
the pressure of time
of dancing feet. cool
lips wisping 'cross
my brow. cool eyes
through the heat

hold me:
i'm falling fast
let's let the smoke hang
let's make forever last

some things I cannot say
some words have no meaning
I want to make this clear
to kiss you might help
might hold off the meanings
but it might not make things clear

a way out of history
please grant me
blinded by light
please take me
blue suspension
empty coffee cups

cars glinting chrome
the radio on

radio:
all plugged in
grooving w you
across the airwaves
in a secret union

L.A.:
all lit up
the nightime gleaming
freeways moving into the city
country estates with guard dogs
freezing in the heat

Don't Look

dont look
DONT LOOK
I want you back
to squeeze
and all night
ride me
I am dusty
I scrape across
you are moisture
glistening brilliant
Ha ha! Brilliance!
I love it!
dont look
dont die
RISE UP

Blue Lights

we see memory unhinge
let fly with huge chords
the past sailing across us.
memory unhinged:
a roomful of bats
a blessing and a curse.
I remember when my
memory returned and the
blue lights faded
some German glimmer girl
standing on the corner
long red hair waving.
the images of next year
wait even now to break loose
to flop on the sand
a damp life-sucking vortex
down and away from me
sticking to the root
of my eye.

Oklahoma/In the Field

Little pools of shade beneath the trees. The bales are
stacked in the hot sun which is like an unbelievable drug.
Dust flying. We end up behind two ancient and dusty
dumptrucks carrying gravel and leaving a thick stream of
particles in the air. Small black pebbles ping-ing off the wind-
shield. Voices have been replaced here by lge billboards,
which speak thru the hot sun. A carny sets up tents on the
flat field of golden grass. The circus is in town. Hot town, hot
time, tonite. We'll send you out in the fields tonight, under
the full moon hanging and the spell of a thousand stars, tiny
spears to the eyes. Or down by that red river at dawn when
mist hangs, just before the heat of day. The barn boards
splinter and crumble of their own volition in this heat. Gray,
crumbling bldgs stand in link w the new. Why tear down any-
thing here where there is so little? Given its chance, the sun
will erase everything here. All history. So we let our heritage
stand, to crumble its own way back to the ground. I look
back on my youth. The fields roll, the clouds roll across
them. I can see for miles, there's no-one in sight.

Yes we're past the deep southwest of cacti and sage now, in
the underbelly of the heartland where golden grasses climb
flat lands with just a trace of roll. Skies here are miles wide,
and the big birds swoop and glide for hours on the lazy cur-
rents. The air is brilliant, etching every detail onto the retina,
threatening to burn thru. The trees hang, the telephone
poles, the sun, the Sun, the SUN!! Over a rise we go. Little
pools of shade beneath the trees!

Electric currents ripple thru the atmosphere. A chill shimmering, a delicate light passes thru me. I am frail, about to break, ready to suffer the winds of change. I see turrets and spires rising up, protecting the farmlands. Carpets of logic blanket the fields. Two small and beautiful blonde children stand at the far end of a row. They don't know about this sky, ready to splinter blue in every direction, ready to sever this orbit, ready to seize their love. Preparing to ignite.

Water towers of assorted odd shapes hang over the landscape like beacons, and giant electric scaffoldings string miles of charged particles over the burnt lakes and summer grasses. The road is ever ahead, snaking its way thru the lives of the people here. Trees pair off and claim space— clusters of apple trees, wild, mix w beech, oak and stands of aspen. Barbed wire and fences are a way of life. The taillights of a big black car fade out of sight, ahead of time, billion year old starlight. The sky is one uniform cloud in this seamless twilight.

There is a man coming out of the tall grass, wiping his hands across his overalls. There are ancient rusted trucks and cars—Plymouths and Chevys, old Fords—around him, w grass sprouting up about the wheels. Long windowless granaries and broken down greying barns, splintered, collapsed. The billboards glow dully today, nothing to say. White paint is peeling and the fields are littered w stones turned up by the glaciers some time ago. Where has he been, coming out from the tall grass? Wiping what stains off his hands in the heat? Down by the lake a fortune is being sold. What does he know of it? His eyes belie his soul, hands over heart. Graying skin belies fierce desires. He moves around the cars, going nowhere. Who's he tryin't kid, in this heat, going nowhere. Hanging around? What's that hung around his waist?

Billboards, bright and faded, sing to me through the heat. Through the rolling gold. Out here the sun is beating down hard, all memory is erased. No-one ever in the sun. The landscape appears deserted. Voices have been replaced by large colorful billboards, fading in the heat. Singing on wavelengths of light.

from **Santa Monica**

every face from the past
is talking at once
in a bar
on the sidewalk
on a side street
in postcards and on
telephone
they're all dressed kinda funny
hands flopping around
i can't see how
they all fit in
where they've come from
where they go
they vanish in thin air
still talking nonsense
still looking for a scheme
to hang life on
still waiting for a vision
a reason to be

saying over and over
tired
drooping
to one person
after the next

"No, I'm not hungry, thanks."
I'm just tired and in need of sleep
In need of some new religion
and a new idea to carry
away from the old things
Not shiny but new
and calm and clear
Not fuzzy
Directed!

To Mary

Mary
a word
a simple word
are you there
in the cold country?
mtns in yr eyes
like a tunnel?
yr mouth still full?
horses galloping
across yr pages?
i'm coming thru
doldrums thru
the trees
to wet sounds
of life. sun
filled rms.
a word just
a word
to mark yr
absence.

In the Kingdom #19

We move along so quickly on roads going nowhere. I ride for hours under the spell of the asphalt. Days, and still end up in the same spot. Inside the same mind. Same life. Same dreams. My body seems to move. My eyes tell me that I move, have motion, and yet my feet have not left their tracks. I am stable—motionless. Unable to take another step. Highways are evil; God is a man standing still, one who knows he is. What kinds of journeys do we expect? Where can we really travel? Some sit complacent, some rush about to grasp at life. Can we travel in our minds? With our bodies, in cars, etc? Cars blasting through space, unaware of the natural world, destroying all in their path. Animals birds cats raccoons dogs people all fall before THE CAR AND DRIVER. Sides of buildings . . . THE CAR AND DRIVER belong to a different species, at odds with life. We must learn the secrets of instantaneous transport. Transportation systems are ludicrous . . .

There was a guy—a forever boy-man touched in the head—who would go around picking up the carcasses of dead animals on the highway. So many, so many unseen from car windows at 60 mph, and he'd take them off and bury them. That much is clear. The first time he found one still panting with the breath of life he took it home with him and, not knowing what else to do, and cared for it. Put a splint on the leg, and bandages. After a while there were quite a few that he'd nursed back to health. Sometimes they left back to the woods, but mostly they hung around his . . . the place he lived. He still went with touched slightly askew reverence to pick up the dead ones, stiff and cold or red and sticky. It was his mission. Somehow without words he knew this. Felt it. Words lead one down certain regular, pre-defined pathways but they can be constricting. Words. Logic. Thought. Reason. Without the words one may have to travel slower, with a candle in the dark instead of hi-beams on the inter-state. Where worlds collide . . . But you move into a different place without words, a special, silent, understanding. He did-n't know any of this—he couldn't think it, yet he knew enough to persevere. With certainty. Unquestioningly. Word-less-ly.

He picked up two one day both living and within half a mile of each other. The distance between us . . . black asphalt hiway recedes . . . converging at the infinite horizon. One of them died on the way, in his hands. He felt neither anger nor remorse, but merely buried it as he did the others.

TAKE THE WHEEL OF THE WORLD and................DRIVE.

They were alive. Like him. He was no better. He did not need words. He did not deny his existence. He moved in daily stasis. Like an animal. Sunrise come. The white rail-ings. The reflective paint. REFLECTIVE PAIN. He walked.

He did what he had to. He asked no questions. He had few conversations. The tar glistens in the noon heat. He tread across the grass, up onto, and down off of, the concrete abutments. Mirage on the highway. Ghosts in the tunnel. The dark cave. Out into the blinding light of the day at breakneck speed. Every bolt rumbling. Glistening highway mirage groans. The slick surface. Careening into first the small mammal, and then screeching along the guardrail, scraping paint and throwing sparks like sheets of pure terror for 400 yards. Over and over, with one final back and forth rocking motion coming to rest, half the front end ripped away, sheared off by the guardrails. The beautiful paint job hope- lessly marred. Smoke and flames.

He moves to the small creature. Searing whistles of steam blowing off, (echoes of the billowy sunlit clouds hi above), oil and other petrol-distillates everywhere, the car on its back, wheels spinning like a cinema classic. A door sags open and a man covered in his own blood drops the three feet or so to the pavement. The car still rattling and shaking as if with a life all its own, unwilling to die. The man—40ish, also after a time, an agonizingly painful unfathomable period of time, time of beyond terror to the dream of reality—is also unwill- ing to die. He realizes this at last.

Suddenly all is quite quiet there in the sunlight, on the high- way. But what? What can I do? I cannot move. Everything is about broken. Blood everywhere mixing with the oil and gas (that other blood). What's moving? Must turn my head. Pain. Unbelievable broken pain. WHITE LIGHT. Blinded. Huh some guy there kneeling in the blinding mirage of white light, all my strength to

'haaaya yuggg oooohh'

Screaming now help me please. He tried to tamp out the bit of burning ember which had leapt from the wreck onto his grimy coatsleeve. Coughing blood. What's happen? He's . . . He's . . . Inching towards final truth. He strode off into the woods with the animal (it still lived), didn't glance back at all.

Still out ghosting the road. Death on the highway. Words crumble around me, and fall with the weight of heaven. I cannot move. I am beneath the great weight. I cannot see. My eyes are blinded. I am in the darkness.

The End of Life in America

the end of life in america
a broken chain of meanings
a torn carpet
that gash in the wall
where the chair flew
dirt under the beds
meaningless headlines
and silence between us
years swallowed up
waiting for something to happen

Angels

mindfuck on the teevee
says you're a jackass
sitting finger-to-button
as unknown teletypes clamor
far off, in my head
they speak of ideas
i haven't yet seen

one million people passed me today
you passed me
eyes to the ground
the dog hadn't been fed all day
and she has strewn the garbage
from the kitchen pail
throughout the house
she starves, and wonders why

your angels are dead
the last of a breed
the sky a hollow tomb now
you can't see it yet
walking the streets
but you'll find out later . . .

death on the hiway
crash on the levee
tears of love
dis-belief
radio eruption
crazy roads running
cruising infinite
auto-dimension
auto-matic freedom
confuse confuse
delude
delude
refute
refrain
black tread in
circles caught
headlight beam-search
explosive glass-shatter
red arclight warning
screaming metal field
dreamland wheel-spin
the flower
the meadow
the hill
proceed with caution
proceed with caution

    *   *   *

images from a child's dream
rising, awake
through sunlit portals
a fallen angel
no longer
in earth orbit
no more
a dark angel
on a stolen ocean
sails up
into the wind
voices reaching
through distant
fingertips of sound
the ideal transfer
from me to you
the crystal encasement
held, locked tight, forever

allow
for a moment
if you will:

the
angels
glide
down

on
wings
of
corten
steel.
wings of victory
that
is
their
feat.

a solitary
thrill
a lonely moment
a dark pool
a damp threat

wish fulfillment

Leap

a leap from the middle
to hold you awhile

swirl, turn, sway, swoop and drop
loop and furl around me moving
houses erupt on ancient, brutal winds
spiritual houses
mommy's houses
splinter boxes
crept over
monuments to lost love
from nowhere to nowhere
in a dream cycle
in a wild light

cross out any larger plans
keep out of vacant lots
beware the strong foundation
eat peaches and apricots

it's razor blade time
ten years of betrayal
shut me off
shut me out
shut me up

Loose/Heat

I hear the beat of drums, the clatter of pool balls on the ancient greens of fast eddie's, the hum of electric current, voltage flowing thru me. A bone-crunching pain. Threatening to level everything, to seal in this world. Life hangs, in danger of being erased. The more you have the more you stand to lose when the fires come burning up to your door. The church steeple looms out and over me and bends in the heat, bursting w the spirits of ancient prayers. On the street headlights gleam. Nobody walks out of this dark heat.

*   *   *

I'm soaked, I love it.
the road rolls, it groans at noon and wraps around the landscape in the evening, the sun setting fireball red under a desert moon.
a moaning moon, cool and electric after midnight.
weeping radiant heat.
majestic arms spread.
indian ghosts on the high ridges.
yellow heat.
my skin, w yr. thoughts.
over the top in my head.
cease in the heat.

skin visions.
electric aces cool us.

my choice suicide:
in the desert
in the heat
scorching across the land.
golden visions invade the mind
bleaching the spirit
pulling six ways at once.
yes, to burn on the way out.

power lines cut the air
we bask in the current
fuzztone/lovetone
we heat up sounds at night

electric whipcrack snap
mental jukebox sailboat
we soak up light
in dark rooms

         *   *   *

things are moving
past the window
in a way more
exquisite

than any movie
could ever be.
the whole green scene
let loose.
all the cool shit
the young planet
the landscape especially
demands to be run through.
I touch the earth
I live mental:
the two sides rebel.
I can't see clear.
I can't see anymore
at all.
We can't belong
because
we don't belong.

So many things now, the things that happen everyday, to
everyone, are hitting me all at once. We're back in the east,
close to people. Kids on the street, little kids, look at me;
they're not sure if they should look me in the eyes, not sure
if they should feel confidence or fear. Afraid to look me in the
eyes, confusion running inside, unprepared for this con-
frontation. Threatened by the unfamiliar. How horrible to
grow up here.

In the Woods

in the woods,
a bird,
a clock that never strikes
we survived the pit
there is a city that sinks,
a lake which rises above it

everything seen:
        visions, gleaming in the air
everything heard:
        the sound of the cities
        in the evening sun
everything known:
        visions, tumult

all the blind stations of life

words burn holes
and fall like lead
only the birds are free
moving high overhead

the past is
automatic
ecstaticall that skin

the spoken word is dead
we mix up confusion
jumble desire and hatred
I touch smooth skin
lap milk from the grass
the desert comes down
blankets fields with heat
as winter moves in
the trees explode
a grenade garage grin
the report from the blast
rushing thru the canyons
the hammer hitting the hand

oceans falter
mountains stiffen
metal fresh ladies
rock the house
smash the windows
come on like the sun
we keep all the lids off
and admit anyone

is the nighttime insane?
peace in our lifetime
is not possible

can the eye hit the target?
can the head feel this tight?
starved like a rocket
like the wind at night

the tide is rising
all history to me
the jigsaw images
the feeling of free.

This Is the Hour of Each Day That Could Last Forever.

Theres nothing happening in the house. Everything is quiet. The light is grey through orange window gauze. Everything seems heavy, full of weight. The girl was slick, she was leanin out over the edge of my chazm, sliding along my rim. The telescope hums softly, wordlessly. My hands are cold and looking old. The phone hasnt rung all day, theres nothing to get over. That girl was slick yeah she was slidin over my rim. I liked her like that, she would catch up to me later.

For the moment everything is slick and smells of you. I can smell yr hair against these walls, when the music is low enough. You are the best witch. The cat yelps when i step on her tail. Theres papers and coffee cups and envelopes and things scattered everywhere here. Im treading about among the debris, waiting for my head to clear, waiting for you to come home. You with all yr slick slippery corners. Come over and hold me tight. Come and press my ribs. Youve got more of what i need than any other girl in the world. I love you for it, im willing to put up with all the shards of debris this life had to offer, just to be near you. Just to smell that smell of yr hair next to my face. I lift yr leg up high and stroke the inside of yr whiteness yr thighs white inside, and run my finger up to yr wet place which feels so nice. You for me you for me now, and now and now . . . Again . . .

In the spring morning we walked along as the trees began to bud and the dogs were all out over the park, you could hear the sounds of construction as they try to build new things. New trees, new grassy lawns that roll like the curves of yr body, of any womans high inside. A guitar sits idle, a moment passes, no thoughts emerge, no bullets fly. This is the hour of each day that could last forever. Im waiting for you to come waiting for you to come waiting for you to come home.

Thoughts grip my mind like a vise, im going to pop out of my head soon, this is the perfect grey day to be home alone laying on the couch and thinking of yr voice. Yr magic box. Yr sharp shoulders. Eyes on fire. Let me slip inside you and clean out my head. Let me empty all my thoughts into you in one full-on surging thrust. Im with you all the time, didnt you know this typewriter has no question mark. How am i possibly going to exist without an end to my questioncccccc

Can i hold your fine ass in front of my face and kiss its so-fine roundnessc can i lean a little too far out yr window and leave this earth with you in towc can we move about these islands of icecc let me play on you drumming my fingers up and down yr lovely skin and feel you all over inside and out, let me remove yr last vestige of doubt. Let me inside yr head so i can let you out.

Telescope/Timeshift

I've been given a glass eye
a hollow telescope
the pavement view
a shadow forming
across fields rushing
through me to you
sharp blade life
sent home
across fields
breathing the earth
a celestial body
high over the city
in flames
a golden moment twisting
thru the city of images
bringing me home

spin me across yr world
lead me on by my desire
I'll stretch out for you
string me up before i cry out
I'm high above the city
dreams distorting
amp thrust full
we belong here
we are safe here

something tells me
the skies are here for us
so brief
so impure

I'm high above the city of images—nothing spoken, every-
thing seen and felt. Each page a picture, every instant anoth-
er world-view. Each image a simple moment in this endless
day. Each day a lifetime of hours, and each lifetime merely a
vague notion, taken from the pages of some old book.

        *   *   *

This last night here is the end of many things. I hold the keys
that tomorrow will fit the locks to other doors. Who knows
what lies ahead? Right now time isn't opening up, it's a rather
stationary thing. Objects and ideas hover about, transfixed in
mid-air, waiting to be taken in hand. Each moment seems to
last forever.

The look in your eyes as I hold their gaze is not a memory,
not a bird in flight, but an endless vision. A tunnel of love, dip-
ping into you. A moment between us lasts forever. File cards
in memory stacked, visions from a dream. Black lace and
high sierras. The cup lies now full, then overturned and run-
ning off.

So much seems to have happened this last month. Another season has drifted by. Feelings of mortality come and go: altering my sense of routine. Exchanging for it an unending madness, an unreality where anything might happen, a time-less zone where nothing happens. Across a line where dreams and waking experiences meet in a cinema of the mind. Nothing less possible than anything else. For instance: I am hovering over a body of golden water, suspended over the clouds. It's not impossible, my eyes are open.

A rushing stream of light: I'm still out walking the Salisbury plain, climbing rocks in Berlin, passing by the Forum in the Roman midnight. Watching trees bud on London streets. These moments all flash-frozen in time, not just my time but all time. Each instant a frame projected outwards, frozen in position and rushing static across the expanse of infinity. Chronos! My man!!

Accomplishment is its own reward. I walk thru a dream punc-tuated by various exorcisms of my soul. Now time will fly by, in a mad dash across Europe. Each image rising and falling on the screen in succession. None lasting, not one holding the moment. I see myself as always, twisting between the image-frames, looking at you and all you do, willing myself not to move. Solid cross-sections of time extend, each one a crystalline gem—splintering off, flipping end over end thru space, outwards and away. This is education! This is life, cut one frame at a time from an endless spool.

I'm In Between Times and Tired of the Wait

254 years
an endless love
yr dark hair
what happened?

N. Carolina
Hemingway
Topless bars
GHETTO BLASTERS
PLANET WAVES
all you want.

I'm talking
1963
THE
BIRTH
OF
TIME

my sister
couldn't be here
my childhood
ended w/ the rain
the river rising

S Wash St
steel bridge
over the river
riding high
over the rushing water

put it all behind me
now it's all behind me

bombarded by sound
love ones neglected
while PAs scream
for all my attention

what is this split
that negates all?
this whirlpool?
this pitchfork?

I can't hear you
These times don't add up.
I can't reach you
These times don't add up.

Don't ask another question
about ten years ago.
Put away the concerns
that keep you up late.
Say so long to the years
that dies behind you.
Goodbye to everyone
that held in the fear.

little pricks on the phone
I was one, remember?
the image of abandon
the tunnel of love
rhthm of the tracks
the sound of a bell

Yr jigsaw image,
now that's the whole of you.
Yr skin and yr hair
rock the street.
the shotgun floor
cushions my head.
I see it
I feel it was at the door

Here it is October
I haven't been home
in six months.
Goodbyes have all been said,
packed up in the trunks.
Dead season jam
all the gears.
The whole thing
has been unloaded.

Scenes 1990

[THESE ARE PICTURE IDEAS; ACCOMPANYING SOUND
WOULD BE MOSTLY NON-SYNC.]

close up: a gun (showing open chambers and shells within).

shot (horizontal) along gun barrel, to trigger, Girl's fingertips,
handgrip, Girl's hand, up her arm to: The Girl.

apartment: Girl hides (or places?–which emotional POV?)
gun in apt. (in a book? a drawer? behind something?).

Girl puts on lipstick, at mirror.

Girl turns on teapot

sits at table leafing through a magazine (table is slightly
strewn), or playing w. the cat, etc.
close-up shots of ordinary things in the apartment

tea kettle whistles finally
Girl pours tea, adds honey, etc.
sits at table w steaming tea

gets up, puts on coat, goes out
(leaves tea steaming in cup)

                    *   *   *

Girl comes out of bedroom
looks out window of apt.
cars, and people, are passing by below her

she turns on TV (it comes up, but no sound)
 or: TV is already on, no sound.

Has a cigarette on couch, puts cig in ashtray
(does not extinguish)
gets up, runs faucet, gets coat, phone rings
cig. smoulders in ashtray
she has an ordinary conversation, which we hear one side of
–nothing special

TV is on, no sound
the room is still
curtains just moving w. the breeze

hangs up phone
(or just sets receiver down?)
grabs coat in a moment
slips out door, leaves apt.

She returns–different clothes, her hair a different color

She strips to lingerie
opens and looks out each window in turn
(there are two or three windows)

she washes her face, etc, in bathroom

lights cig, turns off apt lights
gets in bed
she smokes in bed a moment
red cig ash in the dark

cig gets placed in ashtray (still lit)
we watch the cig burn down, and go out
(in long shot or macro-close-up?)

her breathing slows to sleep-sound

*   *   *

Times Square–midday, looking at the Newsday bldg (with
the news-headlines going around it.

We watch as three or four headlines unfold around it's cor-
ners (and hope for good ones!)

*   *   *

Those tree-shadows in the park here, all whispering, shisk-
ing leaves, around 6 PM, shadows across the cobble-
stones–[shot in NEG–B&W or Color?]

*   *   *

Girl in front of bathroom mirror
she slow and careful paints her face green--
mask-like, or as in Matisse's Portrait w. Green Stripe,
Green & Yellow, with the water running.

[MAYBE THESE LAST THREE SEQU ARE INTERCUT]

*   *   *

Long shot through apt window,
a monologue on top but no Girl in shot

*   *   *

Shots of an empty rain-soaked plaza nearing dusk, bordered
by tall granite bldgs. He waits near a fountain (which is
absurd in the rain) with umbrella–she runs towards him
across the wet courtyard. It's a long, wide shot intercut with
ultra close-ups of puddles reflecting tall bldgs and the foun-
tain, his short cuff and umbrella handle, her dark blue rain-

coat billowing about her as she runs up–the close-ups
almost stop the time of her run up to him –make it seem
frozen in time. She arrives where he is–they speak and ges-
ture for a second (still in long shot). the frenzy which was
somehow evident in both of them a minute earlier suddenly
turns to calm as they speak, we can't see their facial expres-
sions, but even in this long shot we can feel the mood shift
once they connect. In half a minute they kiss, a long embrac-
ing kiss. Then they look about a moment, and hurriedly pull
each other out of the frame, out of the courtyard.

Sound here: rain, distant thunder and car horns, traffic
sounds far off. a dialogue?

*   *   *

The couple enter a movie theatre, shots of them descending
the escalator into the theatre lobby and examining the
posters, the candy stand. They sneak in whilst the attendant
is called away for a moment. We see them file down one
side aisle of the theatre (the left hand aisle) and lean against
the wall. The fillm has begun quite some time ago–they are
observing the audience in their seats instead of the film on
the screen. They whisper together and kiss, and we listen to
them talk as though oblivious to their surroundings–she
relates a story to him of something she overheard that morn-
ing or something she saw transpire in the park, etc. Then
they watch the audience some more, commenting on the

way different aud. members are responding to the film. [It should be a good film, with a good soundtrack behind their talk] He takes out a flash camera and "shoots" the audience, who erupt in protest and annoyance. He apologises, claims an accident. A moment later he triggers the flash again, and the audience becomes very mad, shouting, etc. at the two of them. She's giggling into his collar. The attendant is now coming down the center aisle to see what the fuss is about, they beat a hasty retreat up the aisle, into the lobby, up the escalator and running into the street, look both ways and take off as though nothing out of the ordinary had happened.

Next we see the stills he took, one after the other, with the sound over them which will lead into the next scene.

*   *   *

She's standing on the street near a wall and a guy comes running up, hastily followed by another, they're disheveled and shouting at each other, each holding a can full of house paint. She's caught between them, between fear and fascination, are they arguing or rehearsing a scene? They revolve around her, their bantering back and forth never stops, it's almost as though they don't see her at all. She spins in a circle, watching and listening, spellbound and confused. It ends with the two men flinging the cans of paint high up at the wall, one after the other as each makes his final point, states his final case, etc. Two colors smear and run—she may get splattered but not covered, and she's left there on the street bewildered and casting about (and looking beautiful although now disheveled and flustered too) after they run off. People walking by glance from her to the dripping wall and back again.

*   *   *

A portrait bust of the dark-haired Girl, dressed in black, against a black ground or night/dark scene. She's enigmatic, a serene and beautiful face. She smiles, mugs for the camera, comes running towards it (the backgrounds keep shifting), is thoughtful in profile, addresses the camera, is still like an opalescent skinned statue.

These images are later re-exposed, shooting bright sun points reflecting off the river, so she will sparkle otherwordly, like Peter Pan or a constellation seen on a clear night. The water swirling on top of the images of her, adding a kinetic quality to this section. Maybe also the flashing lights of a police car on the highway at night.

*   *   *

Image of police strobe lights at night along the hiway, coming closer and closer within the frame. What is happening as we pull into viewing range is this: It's two cop cars flashing in strangled unison like some kind of alien craft moored along the guard rail. They've pulled over an early model Chevy pickup, something like that, and a forty-something father is already on the pavement facing the cops and his twenty-something son is stepping out from the passenger's door, in the shadows. What's going on here?

* * *

Image: a field of Queen Anne's Lace, all green and whilte and mid-summer. A Girl is emerging from the field, carrying some strange stuff, like a notebook and a ball-peen hammer, or a straw broom and a battery operated television set (one of those small 5" screens, B&W, ON of course). She's emerging from the fields where a small lane and a large four-lane highway intersect.

* * *

A brief scene of a corousel spinning round, the calliope wheezing, horses going up and down, sunlight dappling over them through some skylights. Some wild shots of this scene from various angles, cut very rapidly, almost to the point of vertigo. Are they in the shot or not? This scene is very rapid fire and brief.

*   *   *

more monologue over
green tree-glade, the color of her face
w. sunlight streaming down
the Girl running (in slo-mo?) through it
in a white dress
from many different angles–
above, below, head on into the camera last.

KODAK VPS 6006   54   KODA

►11

Lee #2

Thom these days I feel so displaced
Nothing feel like anything
There's no room left in this place
I've left my whole life standing

Now I feel so right
And I can't stop dreaming
Now I feel okay
With these thoughts all streaming

Now I feel like an angel
Grown my own set of wings
All the boys are one room dipped in time
And girl you're off in the wind

Now I feel so right
And I can't stop dreaming
Now I am the light
That's what I'm feeling

Now I feel like an angel
With dark eyes shining
Now the world has come undone
No bells are chiming
I'm trying to see this through

To see from me to you
But you can't see me at all
No, you can't see . . . me

I can't stop this now
No, no that's not what I want
And I can't be the one
To calm you down

Thom these days I feel so displaced
Everything here is just television
And I'm left off without a trace
Of the strength of our vision
this dim-lit reason
twilight rhythm
this infinite season
the big decisions . . .

New Sky

a new way to enjoy the sky

i've dreamt this sky of blue
but not this dream of you
not yr hand yr eye

yr delicate complicated gaze
opens new windows
i am back in the spiral
the sea a lost vision
and i must learn to swim again

obscure clouds
genius lore
medication
slo movies
lost angle
empathy
friendship
crooked telephone poles
laughing hysterically

calm and clear
beyond
these fluid thoughts

Mote

When you see the spiral turning for you alone
And you feel so heavy that you just can't stop it
When this sea of madness turns you into stone
A picture of your life shoots like a rocket
All the time

Put "me" in the equation it's alright
I've seen you moving in and out of sight
My friends tell me it'll all cut through you
From nowhere
To nowhere
Cut together
And cutting through

I'm island-bound, a mote inside my eye
I can't see you breathing as before
I am airless, a vacuum child
I can't stand to reason at your door
In this time

If there's a heart to hide in
If there's a rip in this time
If there's a day that lasts
then I'll be fine
If broken bottles shine like jewels

If this decision points to you
If what you say is ever true
Then I'll be fine

I'm down in the daytime out of sight
Comin' in from dreamland I'm on fire
I can see it's all been here before
Dream a dream that lies right at your door

When the seasons circle sideways out of turn
And words don't speak just fall across the carpet
Yr just in time to watch the fires burn
It seems a crime but yr face is bright you love it
All the time

Angels 3

angels, w great iron wings
descend upon me
heavy w ideas
thoughts
dreams

a car is waiting
it's time to go
one true tale is left to tell
one simple sentence waits to be said
one elementary moment

have you heard the word?
have you seen the light?
can you call out the big guns
and blast a hole in the night?

calling off the dogs
the angels delight
sweeping up the dirt
the angels alight

my angel, tonight
dark eyes shining
skin so white

soft spoken
scattered light
let me speak through you
let this come out right
speak the word
to me tonight

brushy, overpainted thoughts
each one on the next
i peel away the layers
the word is you
you stand alone
amongst the angels in
this world tonight.

Lift Off

the big now
waiting to begin
waiting for the word
shading the truth
breaking the light
breathing right into this
this golden time
waiting
re-vision time

WAIT
everyone saying 'wait'
myself repeating the word
WAIT,
hold on tight
let go
spin off the wheel
let go
leave the treadmill

my heart goes out to you
and you
to anyone who will accept
waiting to begin
the handshake

the collar
the thigh
stocking'd feet
understanding NOW
disjointed
thought upon thought
endless echoes
sounding off
sounding right
mate me
shape me
but don't
make me wait

NOW
NOW
I want it
NOW
and
I want it
ALL.

The Midnight Bus

emotions at a fever pitch
waking hours cross into dreams
life like a deck of cards
tossed into the wind

scattered
ecstatic
terrified
lusty
childlike
melancholy
overjoyed

the ground erupting
beneath our feet
every detail in focus

Dublin

morning greens and ancient stonework
conspire to trace memory
time shifts in the breeze
water reflections sabotage
the cadence of the wind
yr grey-blue eyes
her serious brown eyes
his young chocolate gaze
yr. silver skin

turn off memory and
let this train pass through
the sun is silent
the air is brilliant
my eyes are open
my ears are ringing still
w the sound of you

Scottish Dawn

I want to be an artist
I want to be excited
I want to be in ecstasy
I want to be with you

nothing and everything
between us
drifting through
this cut of land
rolling thru
this lemon dawn
holding tight and drifting

plumb the depths of mind
pull up a thought for me
Artist = Reveal-er
expose these frames

open eyes and see:
this aimless rowing
these billboards
this rain
these endless towns
going nowhere
ducking down beneath the bridge arch

rolling flat under aluminum skies
an endless progression
out of the world
this picture revolving
as we stand still

the unlocked box
glittering, revealed
clear and crystaline
mythical
historical
unguided
holding tight
kissing and
closing all gaps
forever-in-a-second

Amsterdam—early morning hotel room

this image i have of yr face by the window
me standing beside you, my arm on yr shoulder
a catalogue of images
flashing glimpses
then gone again

this image i have of yr face by the window
smiling, assured,
stretched out on the bed
this amsterdam morning hotel bed

racing thoughts racing thoughts
people come and go on the street

this image i have of yr face by the window
a hotel in amsterdam
a big fluffy bed
a room with high windows
early morning bells ring lazily on the quarter hour

i see yr hallway dark hallway
i hear yr stairs creak
i can fix my mind
on your 'yes' and your 'no'
i'll film yr face today

in the sparkling canals
all red yellow blue brilliance
and silver dutch reflection

racing thoughts racing thoughts
all too real
you're moving so fast now
i can't hold yr image

i am tethered to this post
that you have sunk in me
in every clear afternoon now
i will think of you:
up, in the air
twisting yr heel
yr knees up around me
my face in yr hair

you scream so well
yr smile so loud
still rings in my ears

FILM DIRECTOR IN MYSTERY DEATH
Thursday, June 10, 1982

Fassbinder's Body is Found in Bed–Munich Police Launch Probe

Cops Rule out Murder

Munich (AP) West German film director Rainer Werner Fassbinder, whose films included "The Marraige of Maria Braun" and "The Desire of Veronica Voss" was found dead today from undetermined causes. A spokesman said Fassbinder, 36, was found in his bed by a woman friend. There was no indication of the cause or time of death. "We do not know if he killed himself or if he took too many pills or too much whisky or something similar," a police spokesman said. "The only thing we are ruling out is murder."

Fassbinder was one of Germany's most talented directors and certainly the most prolific, churning out an average of three or four films a year. His latest film, "The Desires of Veronica Voss"–the tragic tale of a former Nazi starlet who becomes addicted to morphine–won the Golden Bear at the Berlin Film Festival in March. Like many other Fassbinder works, it was widely acclaimed for the technical perfection of its direction and photography.

Fassbinder often shocked the public by openly acknowledging his homosexual relationships and gruff manner. He frequented late-night bars in Munich's bohemian Schwabing district, where he lived, and once was quoted as saying he used cocaine, although he later denied this.

Friends said his brusque, often bizarre manner resulted from early rejection of his work. Fassbinder never forgave the German film establishment for refusing to admit him to the prestigious Berlin Film Academy when he was in his early 20s.

Although his public appearances often suggested a crude nature, Fassbinder's films were filled with sensitivity and sentiment somehow crushed by the weight of circumstance. "The Marraige of Maria Braun," for example–the Fassbinder film most widely seen in the U.S.–told the tale of a young bride left alone in WWII.

Believing her husband missing, she marries an American GI and settles down to struggle through the poverty of post-war life. But her German husband returns. While the two are arguing, Maria Braun, played by one of Fassbinder's favorite actrsses, Hanna Schygulla, goes into the kitchen to light a cigaret from the gas oven. She forgets she has already turned the gas on and dies as soom as she touches the oven ignition. The director's longtime friend, Harry Baer, once said this and other Fassbinder works showed "the price you must always pay for your feelings."

Fassbinder began his professional career as an actring student and director in Munich. Police closed his first theatre down, but the young director, working at the furious pace that characterized his entire career, promptly reopened an "anti-theatre" in another bar. Fassbinders fame began spreading beyond Germany in the early 1970s.

Milano to Turino

a grove of young leafy-green trees, nicely spaced, 10-15 feet
tall, green in gold thatched grass. in the background white
stucco bldgs. blend into the haze of an overcast day, the
gold and green and ochre colors glowing mutely as though lit
from within. meadows filled w brilliant yellow flowers, and
burnt cornfields. an italian woman, late thirties, chesnut
brown hair, blue jeans, black jacket, red cloth gloves red
scarf round her neck walks through the mist, talking aloud to
herself. large trucks roaring by obscure some of what she is
saying. when the trucks are gone all is still.

Koln to Bielefield

what is amazing is how easy it is to discern the minute we cross into germany from holland. the dutch landscape so beautiful, at peace, trees all in straight rows and allees; everything an indication of some sort of harmony.

suddenly we look up and it's obvious we've crossed the border into deutchland. the fence posts shift from relaxed to poised at attention. one can sense a repression, an oppressiveness, just by glancing at the fence posts and the fields, all the tilled dark earth. this has been a constant image of germany for me since my first visit a decade ago–the rich brown tilled earth everywhere–the land so fertile, always in the process of being scored, scarred and dug up as this country's psychology withers beneath the surface, squirming to be free and strong again.

this re-unification business has got everyone, especially the germans themselves, thinking pretty hard, drawing and revising self portraits.

Santa Barbara to L.A.

a new location–the oil derricks along rte 101 south of santa barbara. the stilt legged roads going out into the surf, windswept, to little mounds with a big greasy oil rig, some scrub grass, and a few palm trees. the horizon endless, dotted with other rigs, all around, greasing the water, ancient, black rising towers. we stand talking on the island which holds the rig closest to the shore. the wind is up, the surf is rolling, the sky it's orange, almost sunset. it's an ancient place, how have we come here? it doesn't matter. it's desolate and empty and we feel the same somehow. we are quietly inside the wind, the silhouette hills behind us. what have we got? what is this disease? why do we pull together, only to be pulled apart? what is this way that i feel for you? i know there's a connection here. i know you feel it too.

Tijuana Border

since we spoke from vegas i've written you this letter in my head, now it's finally coming out. these last two days were pretty good out here. i spent last night with some of the guys out shooting pool all night, playing for shots of tequila, which of course made me think of you. needless to say we all got pretty high. this town, in two hours you can walk the length and breadth of it. it's autumn here, beautiful, golden and deep red. in denver there was over a foot of snow!

i can feel you, and taste you, i remember just how we lay together. you and i share ecstasy, not the endless rhythm of monotonous days, but the sparks that can fly.

i'm up til 5 am each night and sleep until noon or one, just sitting up talking, smoking, drinking. it seems easier to think, sometimes, at three in the morning than it does at three in the afternoon while the world is turning. at night it stops, no cars on the street, quiet pools of light on the corners, no chattering talk between the sea and the shore.

Notebook Super 8 Shot List

single strobe face + c.u.
strobe faces
suzanne reading on the bus
flash-lights
rocky desert landscape
strobe-light
flashing lights (long)
john brannon singing, blue then red then to guitarist
fr gtr player (larissa) upwards to pink flashes,etc.
las vegas swirling lights (starts with the moon in the frame)
baghdad teevee
thurston strobe sequ. (w some color shots)
strobe hand (blue sleeve)
sonic youth strobe sequ. (toronto video shoot—b&w)
self portrait still
heart in lights
cody sand castle beach
mote sign
self portrait still (eye)
still frame with hand
tracking foliage shot
"bank berlin" sign
thurston c.u. (mirrorshades)
blurry trees
landscape with steeple and cars moving

(beg w orange/yellow truck passing)green road sign
babes,etc—italian lakeside
tracking italian tree rows
french still life table (color)
self portrait—french window
amanda c.u., at the beach
b+w swirl trees
michelle reading on the bus (2 shots)
spanish candles
kat, c.u., blurred
leaves
candleabra (b&w)
leaves
flag
leaves
cody's walking legs
water ripples
cody + lee at home (b+w)
flashing lights
more cody and lee at home
swirling flashes (starts w pink "grid")
jackie crossing street (red jacket)
"crown" lights (+ stp on stage)
more cody and lee at home—to—windows
hands hiking pants, and telephone
self-portrait moving right offscreen
leah photobooth snapshots (w other flashing images)
kat's shoes

flashing faces (b&w)

yellow driving footage

spanish clips: palms, bldg, tunnel, bldg.

statue

table

door frame-arch, pan up to roof

zoom in on trees

drunk bldgs

swirling abstract bldgs

dog on spanish beach

kids in the water

more water with pregnant mom leading child

night cars, wet road

paris "nuit" sign—2 shots

"cinema" sign

more night cars

checkerboards / "paris" / checkerboards / "by night"

amanda screen porch (waves)

grassy knoll and fire #1

porch still life (color)

grassy knoll and fire #2

susan coming in screen door, pan to floor

vertical leaves

susan, amanda, screen porch (reading road atlas)

leaves

"book/store" signs

lace curtains

green w. fence posts

leaves swirling
guitar strobe
leaves / spinning landscape / leaves
st. louis lamp post lights
st. louis bridges at night
water reflections
wash-out to white leader

end

Fall Tour Film Running Order

color

burroughs—kansas
dallas hotel
burroughs signing books
bus and landscape
hyenas
strobe stuff
hyenas—desolate son
vegas
nighttime reststop—bill and doug
strobe stuff (the hand) + kim
jesus lizard
atlanta nighttime 7-11
florida beach—cody
mote sign
landscape—autumn
toronto video shoot—too dark
sy on stage—too dark
berlin—thurston, travelling shot of trees
focusshot(?) of trees
bus s.p.
landscape footage bdr incl. forest
tv crap
babes in toyland—italian village
italian trees

s. france s.p.(hotel window)
spain—tenements
church candles
flags and leaves
bullfight arena
s.p. on streets
deva—village
180 shot of steve
drunk rooftops
soccer kids
overhead dog
paris by night
dark leaves
bonfire
amanda/susan porch
fall leaves
a + c park
stp stage and lights
s.f.
stp
at home; a-dark, s.p.
scotish stones
driving
souls—roland
yellow driving
carlos
france floods

b&w

at hollywood sign
w. stp—s.f.
nyc—cody hydrant
s.p.—hands, etc
curtains
graveyd.
blurry landscape
souls on stage
t. reading—van
sy on stage—holland?
good t. strobe
michelle on bus
babes on stage
good strobe stuff
paris cafe
candleabra at home
toronto vid-shoot—good
kat on stage—her feet, etc.
xerox s.p.'s—dallas
snapshots
dallas pixillation s.p.'s
landscape
grassy knoll
more good strobe (w. don + lyrissa)
colorado—overexposed lane
dornberg
st. louis bridges + water
c & a.—fla

end

Kurt Obit

8 april 1994
3 a.m.

kurt killed himself. they found his body this morning in his house in seattle. 12 gauge. i had a gig to do tonight with wm. hooker–2 sets. sort of tragic to have to be on stage this night. i didn't have anything particular to say re: death except—what a shame. mtv is a sickness now and is replaying every old clip of kurt they can dredge up and dragging on every soul that held any small piece of his life.

he did it. he was the real thing and we can't follow him now. a true sickness no-one could break through. not even his child could crack the dome of his isolation. how could he come to it? how could he let it take over? a month ago, after rome, i thought he'd become legend, thinking he'd died. now it's the truth. he's left us all behind, here, to puzzle our way into the future. he was doomed to end like this, fame or not. it's all too simple, too real and too complex to fathom.

pray for those that connot believe
pray for the lonely
the aching
the isolated

our thoughts are with you my son
our hopes for your getting over
past words
chants
cities
and all the chatter

get home
get home free
don't let them touch you
don't listen to their talk
save yr soul
let the truth shatter
the shallow methods
the shadowy tv men
get out while you can

why go on?

i understand:
there's nothing left in the music
you've given all you had to give
and now it's time to recognize
all the time that might be spent
getting back somewhere you've already been

so fuck it off
overturn all the pots

leave notes writ in blood
on the walls
to one and all
to family and friends
and all of them

let it go
you're so strong
to let it go
so smart to recognize
the ending

what better day than this?
hair all matted
don't pick up the phone
it's only fake reality
don't answer the door
it's only the gardener
come to trim tired hedges
that are better left wild

Hey Seymour

okay im computerized and
okay it's done
the single i mean

it's not what i thought
but then
it never is

is it?

all is now yrs
free and clear
to have and to hold
and do as you see fit

cover is morley drawings which i will send as well

also h-tarash score
(at last)

so look for it
and let me know
what

      more

            you

                  need.

Toronto

tonight they tore my necklace from my throat as i leaned off-
stage into the crowd during kool thing / got my watch too /
caused me to rip my new trousers while twirling in the strob-
ing pulse / trying to get somewhere long forgotten / striving
to free something nameless, something endless, for awhile /
forcing me to hop for them / hot fire coals beneath my feet
for them / goading me on / holding their breath / paying my
way for things they cannot do themselves / hoping i will fill
the empty hole they feel at the top of their heads / their
pointed little heads / trying to be carried away beneath the
dome, winged statues watching / screaming for more always
more until finally / finally / energy shook free, transferred to
me / keeping me up all night with jittering boundless visions /
they were able to end this day, satiated, and file out into the
cold, maybe leaving with a lover / although mostly children /
able to sleep at last.

HEY OTIS:

I don't know *what/whose* show YOU saw last week, but what I saw was the best show I've seen Dylan do in maybe FIFTEEN years, a MASTER at the height of his POWERS, singing *(singing real good!)* and playing just INCREDIBLY, with a CRACK band supporting him (finally!), playing songs from EV'RY PERIOD of his lengthy CAREER and just doing everything right. I'm talking about before, LONG BEFORE Neil and Bruce came out during 3rd encore and place went ultra-nuts. (When those two were sitting with GINSBERG (& GE Smith) in VIP area, and Dylan was singing *'Only TIME WILL TELL who has fell and who's been left BEHIND',* how could they have felt???) Here he was, just beautiful, singing strong and loud — no mumbles — if you would just stop trying to force the songs to sound like his old vocal stylings and just lissen, fer crissakes, he is doing *really amazing* versions—of MY BACK PAGES, JOEY, BOOTS OF SPANISH LEATHER—songs from ev'ry one of his MANY places and times. Dressed in impeccable black pin-striped western gentleman suit; I felt he'd finally come through, after a decade of alkie/druggie/sexxee troubles and lame shows, he finally seemed ready to assume the mantle which he **RIGHTLY DESERVES** — the same respect that Neil *(f'rinstance)* has. It also occurred to me that in a way his lame shows of recent years past have actually **PROTECTED** him: that his *not* succeeding to be more successful of late has **PREVENTED** him from having to try to get over to ARENA-ROCK size audiences—which of course is the slow death of anybody good. He played fukkin'

ROSELAND! THREE

NIGHTS!!! Hello, Axl? Mad Donna? Oh JaggerKeefHenleyMichaelPink.... Eddie... Stipe... Fukkin WEEZER n SHIT.... *WAKE UP!!!*

Now you know how many Zimmie boots I've got, and you probably also know that I lose most interest 1980 onwards, but maybe, JUST MAYBE it's time to start collecting the '94-5 show pirate copies again.

AMEN! (I like Slow Train Comin' though....)

Now Bob, about producing that next elpee, here's
how I think it should go down...

Kind regards ,

Lee

P.S. In case you were wondering: Neil looked comfortable like he was sittin' in
an old easy chair, he was playing for fun and makin' Bobby laugh; whereas
Bruce couldn't even follow the easy chord changes, all stiff and just watching the
gtr player's hands all through both **Rainy Day Wimmen** (Dylan finally giving the
crowd a real chorus to sing *{EVERYBODY MUST GET STONED!!}* after
confounding their lyrical expectations all night long with brilliant new forms) *and*
Highway 61. How could I have left *this* show (I couldn't), even for **Sebadoh**?

Afterword

What you're holding in your hands is a tight little assemblage of knotty verse and hand held, raw shots of a new mystical road. But not only that.

Road Movies was a catalyst for the copy shop punks who first published it. To me, Susan, and Don, Road Movies was a massive lucky break. It was such an empowering collaboration, its publishing history is a big part of the early history of Soft Skull Press. I'd like to say a few words about that before you turn the final page.

When I think about Lee and Road Movies, I go back to the Kinko's on 24 East 12th Street. Working there was a bright shining hell. The stress was seductive. But at the end of the day I must admit, once or twice it made me weep in my bed. You would look at your life and ask when it would end. The most intense miserable New York customers sought graphic personal validation from a 20-something work crew confused and trapped. We had the brutal realities of capitalist alienation filtered to us through a kindler gentler slackerdom that had no way to express dissent or organize. The wages were pathetic. There were carcinogens and rumors of them in the air. The smells of new Xerox plastic and the funny heat of the Xerox 5090 doing 1000 copies in seven minutes flat were constant companions. But then, because he was friends with Allen Ginsberg, and his young boyfriend David Greenberg, I met Lee Ranaldo one night at the Nuyorican Poets Café. Lee was my hero as a founding member of the radical expressionists Sonic Youth. To me he was the punk, avant, post-Deadhead fauvist poet in one of my favorite bands. He later sent word through young Greenberg that he loved the look of our Todd Colby book Ripsnort. He liked that we made Ripsnort using the machinery around us at the shop. He might have a book of his own. He might be interested in working with us. Are we into it? Yes we are.

Lee started coming into the 12th Street Kinko's. He later wrote about how the customers howling at the barricades reminded him of waiting tables. He came and saw the play I wrote about the swirl of the place, the attempt to make sense of it and organize against its abuses and its relativism. I was seeking after a new expression of the absolute, to the tune of a guitar being beaten with a screw-driver.

Road Movies in manuscript form promised to be a companion to the sonic assault and declamatory monologues already in the fabric of my mind, being a Sonic Youth fan. I first saw them in DC in a huge roller rink with Fugazi in the late 80s. They were teachers in formative years.

The texts of Kim Gordon, Thurston Moore, and Lee Ranaldo outline and encourage resistance. They combine this assertive punk attack and a gutsy pan-tonal artistic experimentation. It's a potent mix and a weapon never more necessary than now. Even the collection of song titles is a manifesto. Kill Yr Idols. Youth Against Fascism. Teenage Riot.

Look at some of the lyrics from the earlier albums. "She's finally discovered she's a . . . he told her so" and the snarly lethal "C'mon get in the car . . . I won't hurt you as much as you hurt me!" Kim Gordon creates a chilling intimacy with the hurtful way males deal with suppressed desire. Patriarchy at the street level with cat calls and child abuse is a social force of oppression. Thurston in on the other side of the marriage between heaven and hell, a "complete inhuman" roiling in guilt. His Catholic upbringing left him with a sense of social justice and the corruption of the Church and State. Prophetic, like Christ himself. Catholic, but with a big block, a big chip, and a big need to jack into the matrix and fix it. Lee's work is less overt, but a perfect complement to the political assault. He lives more on questions of memory and the compelling significance of the past on the present person. Out of chaos he makes a rough poetry. Road Movies fleshes out a new form of humanity that arises from the ruins of capitalism, patriarchy, commercial rock, commodified dissent, and state power.

Without Road Movies, it wouldn't have been possible. Lee was willing to take a chance on a small press, instead of getting a fat advance from a corporate publisher. Right after Sonic Youth's DGC deal, Lee wanted to stay connected to and spread power in the underground. Without Road Movies, Michael Stipe and friends' the haiku year would not have happened. And without the haiku year I wouldn't have been able to land a major national distribution deal with Consortium. That Consortium contract made all the difference when it was time to grow up, set our sites on bigger targets, and publish something controversial about the spoiled rotten Dubya Bush.

Road Movies history as a published book created a story all its own, oscillating and driven like the voice of the poet on the path in these pages. Lee brought the untitled book to us out of his similitude, spiritual generosity, and comradeship. We gave it a name, ran it in multiple small editions, and nurtured it as it nurtured us. May it expand your mind, act like his music, and grow us up past these times of static pollution and smoky ruins.

Sander Hicks
Founder, Soft Skull Press

Lee Ranaldo, musician, writer, and visual artist, is an original member of the group Sonic Youth, formed in 1981 in New York City. They have recorded and performed around the world since that time. Recently three pieces from his HWY SONG series were on exhibit in the show "Go Johnny Go" at the Vienna Kunsthalle, where a Sonic Youth installation—The Destroyed Stage—was also on view. His pieces Madonna Generation and Infinity Feedback Loops were at Gigantic Artspace in New York City in March/April of this year. A new book, Lengths & Breaths—poems long and short, was released by Water Row Press in summer 2004.

Leah Singer is a visual artist whose work ranges from printed matter to film. Copy, the name of her collectible self published newsprint tabloid of silhouette imagery, is an ongoing project that led her to design department store windows and billboard advertising. Her live manipulated film performances have taken her around the globe frequently in a duo with husband Lee Ranaldo. The photographs in Road Movies were culled from various road trips and travels made in the early to mid 1990s at the time the texts were written. The forgotten land-scapes and the poetry of the everyday serve as the visual accompaniment to Lee's wanderlust.